Prayers for Healing

Sammy Cross

Published by Sammy Cross, 2024.

This is a work of fiction. Similarities to real people, places, or events are entirely coincidental.

PRAYERS FOR HEALING

First edition. November 7, 2024.

Copyright © 2024 Sammy Cross.

ISBN: 979-8224968800

Written by Sammy Cross.

Prayers for Healing
Focused prayers for physical, emotional, and spiritual healing.

In a world where physical, emotional, and spiritual struggles are part of our daily journey, healing often feels like a distant hope, reserved for times that may never come. Yet, within each of us lies a profound desire for restoration—to be whole, to feel peace, and to find strength and solace beyond our own. Prayers for Healing was created with this deep yearning in mind, bringing together 120 beautifully crafted prayers to support, uplift, and renew.

Each prayer in this collection serves as a unique pathway to healing, inviting readers to enter a space where faith and comfort converge. Whether you are seeking physical restoration, emotional release, or a spiritual rekindling, these prayers are written to meet you exactly where you are. Each one speaks to specific areas of need, from overcoming fear to finding strength in illness, from healing broken relationships to letting go of past hurts. No matter what you carry in your heart, these words offer a soft place to land—a reminder that healing is a journey, and you are not alone in it.

In our most challenging moments, we often seek words to express our longing, our hope, our gratitude, and our faith. The prayers within this book were crafted not only as expressions of faith but as beacons of light to guide you toward peace. Accompanied by thoughtful reflections and scriptures, each prayer invites you to connect with God's healing presence and to embrace the comfort and renewal that faith can bring.

May this book serve as a companion, a source of strength, and a reminder that healing is possible through prayer, patience, and trust. Let each word breathe new life into your spirit, bringing you closer to the peace, joy, and wholeness you seek. Whether you open this book in times of struggle or gratitude, may you find grace on every page and hope in every line.

Welcome to your journey of healing.

Prayer for Renewed Strength in Body and Spirit

Heavenly Father, I come before You in need,
Seeking Your healing, Your strength, indeed.
My body is weary, my spirit worn thin,
I ask for renewal deep within.
Touch my limbs with Your healing hand,
Grant me the strength to rise and stand.
Restore the energy that's lost and gone,
And give me courage to carry on.
May Your love infuse each cell and vein,
Relieving all weakness, washing away pain.
Lift me, Lord, from this valley low,
So Your strength within me brightly shows.
With faith I ask, in Jesus' name,
That health and wholeness I reclaim.
Thank You, God, for hearing my plea,
And restoring vigour to body and me.

Prayer for Healing and Wholeness

Lord, You know the struggles I face,
The battles with illness and weakness I trace.
I ask for wholeness in every way,
For physical strength, come what may.
Touch my body, remove the strain,
Release me from this lasting pain.
May every cell be filled with light,
Restoring health, making things right.
Guide the doctors who treat my need,
Let every treatment Your wisdom heed.
I trust in You, my Healing King,
For all the peace and hope You bring.
Thank You, Father, for Your grace so true,
I place my health and heart in You.
Restore my body, make me whole,
With wellness flowing, soul to soul.

Prayer for Recovery After Surgery

Loving God, I am grateful today,
For guiding me through in every way.
The surgery's done, the healing begins,
I trust You, Lord, for strength within.
Ease the soreness, soothe the pain,
May my body rebuild, my health regain.
Bless the wounds with tender care,
Healing me fully, beyond compare.
I lean on You in this time of rest,
Knowing Your plan for me is best.
May every moment draw me near,
And in Your love, let go of fear.
Thank You, Lord, for seeing me through,
For holding me close, my strength in You.
With each new day, I'll rise again,
Grateful for life—Amen, amen.

Prayer for Energy and Vitality

Lord, my strength feels far away,
I need Your power anew today.
I ask for energy, vibrant and real,
A Vigor only You can reveal.
Breathe into me, life anew,
That I may stand, my purpose true.
Release fatigue, lift all strain,
Bring health and joy in Your name.
May every part of me be whole,
From weary limbs to tired soul.
Refresh, restore, make me strong,
With You, my God, I belong.
Thank You, Lord, for Your touch so kind,
For healing both my body and mind.
I trust in You, my endless supply,
And lift my voice to glorify.

Prayer for Peace Amidst Physical Struggle

Lord, give me peace as I walk this path,
Strength to endure and joy in my heart.
Though my body struggles, weak and frail,
In Your love, I will not fail.
Let Your calm replace all dread,
Fill my soul with peace instead.
Guide me through each day anew,
Knowing my strength is found in You.
Thank You, Lord, for Your endless grace,
For holding me close in Your embrace.
In body and spirit, make me whole,
Restoring comfort, peace, and soul.

Prayer for Renewal and Restoration

Dear God, I lift my hands to You,
Seeking strength and life anew.
Refresh my body, heal each part,
Mend every ache, soothe my heart.
Renew in me a vibrant fire,
A strength that never will tire.
Let Your love bring health complete,
With faith unshaken, firm, replete.
Thank You, Father, for all You give,
In Your grace, I rise and live.
May every fibre be restored,
In You, my Savior, my King adored.

Prayer for Overcoming Pain

Lord, You see the pain I bear,
The heavy burden I cannot share.
I ask for relief, for strength to endure,
In Your healing, I am secure.
Touch my body, ease each ache,
Grant me rest when I am awake.
Release the tension, calm my soul,
And make my weary spirit whole.
Thank You, God, for all You do,
Your love, unwavering, ever true.
I hold to hope, I trust Your plan,
In You, my strength, my healing span.

Prayer for Patience in Healing

Father, grant me patience here,
To wait with faith, to know no fear.
Though healing may take time to show,
Your love is with me, this I know.
Teach me trust as days go by,
Lift my heart and hear my cry.
Help me see the growth in pain,
To know that healing's not in vain.
Thank You, God, for time You give,
To heal, to strengthen, and to live.
I rest in You, my hope, my friend,
With patience strong until the end.

Prayer for Strength through Chronic Illness

Lord, my journey seems so long,
I need Your strength to carry on.
In chronic pain, I lose my fight,
But in Your power, I find light.
Uphold me, God, with steady grace,
In every hardship, show Your face.
Teach me strength that endures and stays,
Through challenging nights and wearied days.
Thank You, Lord, for love profound,
For peace in trials, solid ground.
My trust is anchored, firm in Thee,
In life, in pain, eternally.

Prayer for Rejuvenation and Recovery

Gracious God, revive my soul,
Heal my wounds, make me whole.
Pour into me Your boundless grace,
And fill me up in this quiet place.
Restore my body, mind, and heart,
With each new day, a fresh restart.
Bring wellness, Vigor, strength anew,
That I may live each day for You.
Thank You, Lord, for hearing my plea,
For Your faithful love surrounding me.
In every breath, may healing flow,
With gratitude, my spirit grows.

Prayer for Release from Pain

Lord, in my pain, I seek Your care,
A soothing touch, a gentle prayer.
My body aches, my spirit weeps,
In faith, I trust the peace You keep.
Take this pain, this heavy load,
And guide me on a peaceful road.
With every breath, let healing flow,
In Your presence, let comfort grow.
Give me strength to bear each day,
And grace to face the things I pray.
Fill me with peace from head to toe,
And let Your mercy overflow.
Thank You, Lord, for love so kind,
For peace that fills both heart and mind.
In You, my soul finds sweet release,
And in Your presence, perfect peace.

Prayer for Comfort in Times of Pain

God of comfort, hear my plea,
As I come to You, on bended knee.
My body is weary, my spirit worn,
From this pain, I feel so torn.
Wrap me in Your arms of care,
And lift the burdens I must bear.
Calm my heart and ease my strife,
Renew in me the gift of life.
Guide me through each aching hour,
With strength drawn from Your healing power.
Let comfort flow like gentle rain,
And free my soul from endless pain.
Thank You, Lord, for hearing me,
In Your love, I find tranquillity.
With faith I rest, my worries cease,
Held in the safety of Your peace.

Prayer for Strength Amidst Suffering

Lord, I feel so weak and frail,
Through endless nights, my strength grows pale.
In times of pain, draw near to me,
Your healing love, my remedy.
Grant me courage, fill my heart,
As from this pain, I pray to part.
Let hope arise as I hold on,
To face each day, until it's gone.
In Your strength, I'll find my way,
Enduring pain with grace each day.
Hold me close, my Shepherd true,
For I find peace when I'm with You.
Thank You, Lord, for love divine,
In my weakness, Your strength shines.
With faith I rise to face the test,
In Your embrace, I find my rest.

Prayer for Peace in the Midst of Pain

Dear Lord, my soul cries out in need,
For peace and calm, a gentle lead.
Amidst the pain that holds me tight,
Bring forth Your healing, Your holy light.
Let comfort fall upon my soul,
And make my broken body whole.
Calm my heart with peace so pure,
That I may find the strength to endure.
Guide my thoughts to higher ground,
Where hope and faith in You abound.
Even in pain, I find my peace,
In Your love, my fears release.
Thank You, Lord, for peace so sweet,
For making me whole, from head to feet.
With every prayer, my spirit grows,
In Your presence, my comfort flows.

Prayer for Gentle Relief from Pain

Father, with hands uplifted high,
I seek Your grace, my spirit's sigh.
My pain is heavy, hard to bear,
But I know You hold me with tender care.
Soften the edges of my ache,
And in Your comfort, let me wake.
Breathe Your peace into my soul,
And make my broken body whole.
Let every part of me find rest,
In Your love, I am truly blessed.
Release this burden, make me free,
As I surrender all to Thee.
Thank You, Lord, for hearing my call,
For holding me when I might fall.
With gentle love, You take my hand,
And guide me toward Your promised land.

Prayer for Restful Sleep Amid Pain

Lord, as I lay my head tonight,
I ask for peace, a soft, sweet light.
Pain has lingered through the day,
But in Your love, I find my way.
Grant me rest, undisturbed and deep,
That I may find a healing sleep.
Let every ache and throbbing cease,
And fill my dreams with calming peace.
Protect my heart, renew my mind,
In Your arms, rest I find.
With faith, I close my eyes to see,
The comfort that You give to me.
Thank You, Lord, for being near,
For every whispered word I hear.
In You, my soul finds perfect rest,
My healing Savior, I am blessed.

Prayer for Hope During Chronic Pain

God of hope, my heart is weak,
With words of comfort, let me speak.
For in this pain, I struggle to cope,
Yet in You, I find my hope.
Though chronic pain may linger long,
In You, I find my courage strong.
Hold me close, ease my fears,
And dry the sadness of my tears.
Grant me hope to face each day,
In Your light, I'll find my way.
Your love sustains, Your strength upholds,
In You, a brighter future unfolds.
Thank You, Lord, for hope divine,
For being with me, every time.
With faith I wait, my spirit free,
For Your healing love surrounds me.

Prayer for Comfort in the Quiet Moments

Lord, in the silence, I feel my pain,
The weight, the ache, the lasting strain.
Come to me in these quiet hours,
With healing grace, let comfort flower.
Let Your peace flow like a stream,
Through every thought, through every dream.
Ease my body, calm my mind,
In You, true solace I find.
Though I may suffer, I'll trust in You,
For strength to carry me through.
Each silent prayer, You hear, You know,
In Your embrace, my comfort grows.
Thank You, Lord, for being near,
For calming every anxious fear.
With faith, I rest, my pain released,
In Your love, I find my peace.

Prayer for Easing of Painful Days

Heavenly Father, hear my cry,
As painful days and nights go by.
I long for relief, for strength anew,
I lift my hands in prayer to You.
Let every ache and weariness cease,
Replace my pain with perfect peace.
In Your mercy, take my pain,
And let my spirit rise again.
Teach me strength that endures each day,
With hope to guide me on my way.
Hold me close, my loving friend,
Your healing touch, my heart's mend.
Thank You, Lord, for Your embrace,
For comfort in this sacred space.
With faith I wait, my pain subsides,
In You, my joy and peace abide.

Prayer for Strength and Resilience in Pain

Father, grant me strength and grace,
To face this pain, to find my place.
Though my body may feel weak,
In Your arms, my hope I seek.
Help me bear each trying day,
With resilience in every way.
Let Your power sustain my soul,
And in Your love, make me whole.
Though I may struggle, You are near,
To calm my pain, dispel my fear.
Guide my heart, make me strong,
In Your love, I belong.
Thank You, Lord, for strength to bear,
For lifting me in love and care.
With faith renewed, I rise each day,
In Your healing, I find my way.

Prayer for Peace in Anxious Moments

Lord, my heart is filled with fear,
I feel the weight of worry near.
Anxiety grips, my mind won't rest,
In Your peace, I seek my best.
Calm the thoughts that race within,
Help me let go, let peace begin.
Fill me with Your gentle grace,
And in my soul, make fear erase.
When panic rises, bring me still,
Let me trust in Your perfect will.
Hold me close, my guiding light,
Through darkest times, be my might.
Thank You, Lord, for peace You give,
In Your love, I truly live.
With faith in You, my fears release,
In Your arms, I find my peace.

Prayer for Courage to Face Fear

Dear God, when fear is all I feel,
Help me trust that You are real.
When doubts arise and courage fades,
Shine Your light through anxious shades.
Make me brave to face each day,
And help me trust in what You say.
Guide my steps when paths are dim,
And hold me close, for fear is grim.
Give me strength to stand and fight,
To trust in You with all my might.
For You are greater than my fear,
In Your presence, You draw near.
Thank You, Lord, for courage strong,
In Your arms, I now belong.
With faith in You, my heart can soar,
And fear will haunt me nevermore.

Prayer for Inner Calm

Father, calm my racing heart,
In Your peace, let worries part.
Take this anxious mind of mine,
And let Your healing spirit shine.
In every breath, I seek Your grace,
To steady me in this fearful place.
Fill me with Your calm, divine,
And make Your presence truly mine.
When storms of fear begin to rise,
Lift my spirit to clearer skies.
Let every worry fade away,
And in Your peace, I choose to stay.
Thank You, Lord, for calm so true,
For comfort found in knowing You.
With faith, I trust, I will not break,
In Your embrace, my peace I take.

Prayer for Trust Over Worry

God, help me trust beyond my sight,
When fear creeps in, dark as night.
Replace each anxious thought I bear,
With hope and trust, beyond compare.
Teach me faith in all You do,
To walk in peace, close to You.
Calm my heart, let trust abide,
In every fear, be by my side.
Though worry tries to cloud my way,
In Your light, let courage stay.
Help me see Your hand so near,
And trust in You instead of fear.
Thank You, Lord, for faith so pure,
In You, my confidence is sure.
With peace, I rise above each dread,
And walk with You where hope is led.

Prayer for Resilience Against Anxiety

Lord, grant me strength to stand today,
When anxiety tries to lead me astray.
Build in me a courage strong,
And help me know that I belong.
In moments dark, make me bold,
In Your truth, let fear unfold.
Guard my mind, protect my heart,
And let Your wisdom not depart.
Though worry tempts me to despair,
I lift my eyes, for You are there.
With every breath, I'll stand secure,
In Your love, I will endure.
Thank You, Lord, for strength to bear,
For peace beyond what fears declare.
With You, my heart will rest at ease,
In Your calm, my worries cease.

Prayer for Freedom from Fear

Heavenly Father, hear my cry,
As fears around me multiply.
In anxious thoughts, I feel confined,
Bring me peace of heart and mind.
Break the chains that hold me tight,
And guide me through to morning's light.
Fill my soul with calm so true,
And make me brave to trust in You.
For in Your hands, I am safe,
In Your presence, fear will chafe.
With You, my soul can rest secure,
Your love for me is ever pure.
Thank You, Lord, for setting free,
The anxious heart inside of me.
With faith renewed, my soul will rise,
In freedom found, my spirit flies.

Prayer for Serenity of Mind

Lord, I need Your gentle hand,
In moments hard to understand.
When anxious thoughts begin to grow,
Help me breathe, help me know.
Guide me through this darkened haze,
With peace that fills and hope that stays.
Take away the thoughts that bind,
And grant me a serene mind.
With every breath, let calm increase,
In Your love, I find release.
Teach me stillness, deep and true,
To find my strength, my peace in You.
Thank You, Lord, for peace divine,
For helping me leave fears behind.
With faith, I stand, my soul complete,
In Your embrace, anxiety retreats.

Prayer for Healing from Worry

Father, heal this worry deep,
Release me from its hold so steep.
In every anxious thought I bear,
Let me find Your comfort there.
Help me surrender fear to You,
In Your hands, all things are true.
Teach me trust that runs so deep,
That in Your peace, my soul may sleep.
Thank You, Lord, for rest You bring,
For calming every worry's sting.
With faith, I know my heart will mend,
And in Your care, my worries end.

Prayer for Confidence Over Fear

Lord, instil within my heart,
A confidence that won't depart.
Though fear may try to take control,
Help me know my fearless role.
In every doubt, let faith arise,
For in You, no fear applies.
Guard my heart, shield my soul,
Make Your confidence my goal.
Thank You, Lord, for courage clear,
For helping me release my fear.
With trust in You, I walk secure,
And in Your love, my heart is pure.

Prayer for Lasting Peace

Lord, I seek Your lasting peace,
That all my anxious thoughts may cease.
Bring me calm that won't depart,
And heal my worried, restless heart.
Help me dwell in perfect rest,
Knowing I am truly blessed.
With every breath, let peace arise,
And drive the fear that blinds my eyes.
Thank You, Lord, for peace so pure,
For calming fears I can't endure.
With faith, I trust, I will not fall,
In Your love, my heart stands tall.

Prayer for Healing Past Hurts

Lord, I bring my past to You,
The hurts and wounds, both old and new.
With gentle hands, please heal each scar,
And take away the pain held far.
Release the memories that cause me pain,
And let Your peace within me reign.
Touch every part, each wound unseen,
And make my spirit pure and clean.
With each deep breath, let healing flow,
In Your presence, let mercy grow.
May I forgive and find release,
To live again in perfect peace.
Thank You, Lord, for healing grace,
For helping me my past erase.
With faith in You, my heart renews,
And I find strength to face what's true.

Prayer for Letting Go of Painful Memories

God, I need Your loving hand,
To help me let go and firmly stand.
The memories linger, they pull me back,
Along a long-forgotten track.
Release me from this binding chain,
And heal each trace of lingering pain.
Fill me with peace, remove the weight,
Help me live with a heart that's straight.
In Your strength, I rise anew,
To leave the past and walk with You.
With each step forward, may I heal,
In Your love, let peace be real.
Thank You, Lord, for letting me see,
That You have set my spirit free.
With faith, I trust in what's ahead,
With You, I walk where hope is led.

Prayer for Healing from Betrayal

Lord, You know the pain I feel,
From wounds of trust that need to heal.
Betrayed and broken, I come to You,
For comfort, peace, and strength anew.
Touch my heart and make me whole,
Mend the pieces, soothe my soul.
Teach me grace to forgive in time,
And help me leave the hurt behind.
Though trust may falter, You remain,
My steady rock amidst the pain.
In Your love, I find my way,
Through darkest nights to brighter day.
Thank You, Lord, for healing deep,
For holding me when I cannot sleep.
With faith, I trust in love again,
In You, my healing will begin.

Prayer for Healing Childhood Wounds

Father, You know my childhood's tale,
The moments where I felt so frail.
The wounds from years I cannot change,
The scars that still feel strange.
Heal the child within my heart,
Give peace that never will depart.
Let Your love replace each ache,
And give me joy for my soul's sake.
Guide me through the hurt I hold,
With gentle care, make me bold.
Help me forgive, release the past,
To find the peace that truly lasts.
Thank You, Lord, for being near,
For lifting me above my fear.
With faith, I rise, my heart is free,
In Your embrace, my soul will be.

Prayer for Overcoming Grief and Loss

Lord, my heart is burdened sore,
From grief and loss I can't ignore.
Comfort me, O gentle King,
And help me find the peace You bring.
Hold me close, wipe every tear,
Let Your presence calm my fear.
Release the sorrow in my soul,
And make my broken spirit whole.
With each day, renew my strength,
To find my joy, to go the length.
Though grief remains, I trust in You,
To guide me gently, lead me through.
Thank You, Lord, for love so pure,
For peace that helps my heart endure.
With faith, I walk this path of pain,
In You, I find my hope again.

Prayer for Releasing Guilt and Shame

God, I carry guilt and shame,
A weight I cannot fully name.
Please lift this burden from my heart,
And grant a fresh and healing start.
Forgive my past, forgive my wrong,
Make my spirit brave and strong.
Let mercy flow like healing rain,
And wash away each trace of pain.
Help me leave my shame behind,
With love so pure and peace refined.
In You, I find my worth anew,
With grace that makes my heart true.
Thank You, Lord, for freedom's light,
For breaking chains and ending night.
With faith, I stand, redeemed and whole,
In Your grace, I free my soul.

Prayer for Forgiving and Letting Go

Lord, the hurt I hold is deep,
A wound that never lets me sleep.
Help me forgive, to let love grow,
To find release and let it go.
Give me grace to heal the pain,
To see beyond what wounds contain.
In Your love, help me forgive,
And let compassion truly live.
Grant me strength to choose what's right,
To walk with love and faith in sight.
With every breath, let peace replace,
The hurt and sorrow I embrace.
Thank You, Lord, for setting free,
The heart that seeks Your liberty.
With faith, I rise above the pain,
And find in You, my peace again.

Prayer for Restoring Joy After Trauma

Father, joy feels far away,
My heart feels cold, in disarray.
Restore the joy that once was mine,
With light that heals, with love divine.
Breathe Your peace into my soul,
And make my broken spirit whole.
Let laughter find a way to bloom,
To fill the silence, heal the gloom.
Guide me through each healing step,
In Your care, my soul is kept.
Help me find the joy to live,
With grace to heal and strength to give.
Thank You, Lord, for joy so sweet,
For laughter's sound, for love's repeat.
With faith, I rise, my heart anew,
In You, my joy is pure and true.

Prayer for Emotional Resilience

God, I need resilience strong,
To heal the wounds I've carried long.
Help me find the strength to heal,
To open up, to let love feel.
Take my burdens, take my fears,
Hold my sorrow, dry my tears.
Teach me courage, teach me grace,
To rise above in this holy space.
Though memories may still remain,
Help me find peace beyond the pain.
With You, I rise to heal and grow,
In Your light, let wholeness flow.
Thank You, Lord, for strength You give,
For hope renewed, for love to live.
With faith, I walk, my spirit free,
In Your embrace, my liberty.

Prayer for Healing from Heartbreak

Lord, my heart feels torn apart,
From love that's left a wounded heart.
I seek Your touch, Your healing grace,
To mend the scars, to fill the space.
Restore in me a heart made whole,
Remove the pain that took its toll.
Help me love and trust anew,
With faith and courage born of You.
Though love was lost, I hold to this,
In Your embrace, I find my bliss.
Heal each tear and mend each scar,
With love that reaches near and far.
Thank You, Lord, for love divine,
For making this broken heart mine.
With faith, I trust, my soul restored,
In Your healing, I am adored.

Prayer for Restoring Faith

Lord, I come with a weary heart,
Feeling distant, worlds apart.
My faith feels faded, hard to find,
Renew my soul, my heart, my mind.
Shine Your light within me now,
Restore my faith, show me how.
Let doubts be gone, let strength arise,
And lift my gaze to clearer skies.
Draw me near and keep me close,
Fill my spirit with Holy Ghost.
In You, I find my purpose true,
A life of faith, renewed in You.
Thank You, Lord, for faith restored,
For drawing me back to Your word.
With every prayer, my soul will sing,
In You, I find my everything.

Prayer for Renewing My Spirit

Father, my spirit feels so low,
I need Your strength, Your light to show.
Revive my heart, renew my soul,
Make every broken part feel whole.
Let Your presence fill this place,
With holy love and boundless grace.
Guide me through this season long,
Make my spirit brave and strong.
I seek Your touch, Your healing balm,
To fill my soul with peace and calm.
With every breath, may faith restore,
And lead me closer, more and more.
Thank You, Lord, for strength anew,
For peace that flows and faith so true.
In You, my spirit finds its way,
Renewed in love, day by day.

Prayer for Finding Purpose Again

God, I feel so lost inside,
Wandering with no guide.
Bring me purpose, make it clear,
Show me why You placed me here.
Let Your wisdom light my path,
And quiet all my doubts and wrath.
Help me see the plan You've laid,
And trust in You, unafraid.
In Your presence, may I grow,
The purpose only You can show.
Give me strength to walk the road,
And carry my spiritual load.
Thank You, Lord, for purpose pure,
For faith in You, my heart's secure.
With You, I'll walk the path anew,
In purpose found, my strength is true.

Prayer for Strength in Times of Doubt

Lord, I'm wrestling with my doubt,
With questions I can't sort out.
Help me trust and not despair,
And feel Your presence everywhere.
When my faith feels weak and frail,
Be my strength, let hope prevail.
Guide me through these shadows deep,
And in Your love, my spirit keep.
Let doubt become a pathway bright,
To deeper faith and greater light.
I trust in You, I won't let go,
For in Your truth, my heart will grow.
Thank You, Lord, for steadfast grace,
For guiding me in this sacred space.
With every step, I'll trust and see,
Your love is all I truly need.

Prayer for Restoring My Connection with God

Father, I long to feel You near,
To sense Your voice, Your presence clear.
Renew the bond that once was strong,
And let my soul sing a holy song.
Let nothing stand between us, Lord,
For I am Yours, my heart restored.
In quiet moments, help me see,
The love You've always given me.
Draw me closer every day,
Teach me how to trust and pray.
In You, my strength and comfort lies,
As I feel Your spirit rise.
Thank You, Lord, for love so deep,
For promises You always keep.
With faith renewed, my spirit's whole,
In You, I find my heart and soul.

Prayer for Spiritual Renewal and Fresh Vision

Lord, my vision feels so blurred,
I need Your clarity, Your word.
Give me eyes to truly see,
The path You've set ahead for me.
Renew my spirit, cleanse my mind,
In Your wisdom, make me kind.
Let love and grace be my guide,
With faith and purpose by my side.
Strengthen me to walk in light,
And banish every shadowed fright.
With vision clear, I'll walk with You,
In steadfast faith, in purpose true.
Thank You, Lord, for sight restored,
For guiding me back to Your word.
In Your love, my vision's whole,
Renewed in strength, in mind and soul.

Prayer for a Heart on Fire for God

Father, ignite my heart today,
Fill me with a passion that will stay.
Let my love for You burn bright,
And fill my soul with holy light.
Where apathy and doubt have grown,
Let seeds of faith be clearly shown.
Renew my spirit, light the flame,
That I may live to praise Your name.
In every step, let love abound,
For in Your grace, my life is found.
With joy and purpose, let me soar,
To love You deeply, evermore.
Thank You, Lord, for love's pure fire,
For passions bright that never tire.
In You, my heart is fully whole,
My spirit burning, filled with soul.

Prayer for Reawakening My Faith

Lord, awaken faith in me,
To see the world as You would see.
Remove the veil that keeps me bound,
And in Your light, let faith be found.
Strengthen me to walk Your way,
To trust and follow every day.
Give me faith that stands so sure,
Through every trial, pure and pure.
In Your truth, let doubts depart,
Fill every corner of my heart.
With faith unshaken, firm and strong,
I'll live in You, where I belong.
Thank You, Lord, for faith anew,
For every moment spent with You.
With faith unbreakable, I rise,
In Your love, my spirit flies.

Prayer for Drawing Closer to God

Father, bring me near to You,
Let my spirit feel anew.
Draw me closer every day,
Guide me in Your holy way.
Help me listen, help me hear,
For in Your love, I have no fear.
In quiet whispers, speak to me,
And set my wandering spirit free.
In every moment, help me find,
A deeper love, a faith aligned.
With each step, I'll follow near,
With You, my soul is held so dear.
Thank You, Lord, for drawing me close,
For every blessing You bestow.
In Your presence, I'm complete,
My heart renewed, my life replete.

Prayer for Spiritual Refreshment

Lord, my soul feels parched and dry,
I long for You, my spirit's cry.
Refresh me with Your holy rain,
And heal my heart of every strain.
Pour out Your love, Your peace, Your grace,
And let me rest in Your embrace.
Revive my heart, renew my mind,
In You alone, my strength I find.
May Your spirit flow like streams,
Bringing life and sacred dreams.
With every drop, my heart will grow,
In Your love, my spirit glows.
Thank You, Lord, for streams of grace,
For lifting me in this quiet space.
With faith renewed, I rise once more,
In You, my soul will soar.

Prayer for Restoring Broken Bonds

Lord, I come with a wounded heart,
From broken bonds that drift apart.
In Your grace, please heal the pain,
And let love's light shine once again.
Where words have hurt and trust has waned,
Restore the bond that once remained.
Grant me courage to forgive,
And in Your love, teach me to live.
Bring us close and heal each scar,
Help us see how loved we are.
In every hurt, let grace abide,
With open hearts on either side.
Thank You, Lord, for love's repair,
For softening hearts through earnest prayer.
With faith in You, we'll start anew,
In bonds restored, deep and true.

Prayer for Healing a Friendship

Father, You know the loss I feel,
From a friendship that once was real.
Guide us both to understand,
And reconcile with love's command.
In every hurt and unkind word,
Help healing grace be seen and heard.
Teach me kindness, teach me grace,
To mend the wounds and find our place.
If this friendship be Your will,
Help us love each other still.
Bring back the trust, renew the bond,
Let us move together, strong.
Thank You, Lord, for friendship dear,
For healing hearts and drawing near.
With faith, we'll walk this road again,
In You, our friendship shall remain.

Prayer for Reconciliation in Family

Lord, within my family's heart,
So many wounds have torn apart.
Help us find the way to heal,
To speak the love we truly feel.
In every word that caused a tear,
Bring understanding, draw us near.
Help us forgive, let go of pride,
And let compassion be our guide.
Where anger dwells, let peace replace,
Let mercy fill this sacred space.
Restore the bonds that time has worn,
And help us all be reborn.
Thank You, Lord, for family ties,
For helping us to empathize.
In Your love, we find our way,
And build anew, day by day.

Prayer for Restoring Trust

Father, trust is hard to gain,
Once it's lost, there's lingering pain.
Help us rebuild what's been torn,
With love and patience, newly born.
Give us courage to believe,
To offer grace, to not deceive.
Let honesty and truth abide,
In every step we walk beside.
Teach us faithfulness and care,
And let Your love replace despair.
In trust renewed, let healing flow,
So stronger bonds of love may grow.
Thank You, Lord, for trust restored,
For guiding us with Your accord.
With faith in You, our trust will stand,
In Your love, hand in hand.

Prayer for Healing After Hurtful Words

Lord, harsh words have caused a tear,
And left behind hurt everywhere.
Help us mend what words have done,
And let forgiveness be begun.
Teach me, Lord, to speak with grace,
And heal the wounds I cannot trace.
Where hurt has dwelled, let peace begin,
Restore our love, remove our sin.
May we listen, may we care,
With softened hearts, our burdens share.
In love renewed, let grace increase,
And fill our souls with perfect peace.
Thank You, Lord, for love's repair,
For teaching us to treat with care.
With faith in You, we'll make amends,
And build our love that never ends.

Prayer for Compassion in Relationships

God, give me eyes to truly see,
The pain of those who walk with me.
Fill my heart with empathy,
To show compassion tenderly.
Help me understand their fears,
And wipe away the hidden tears.
Teach me grace to speak with love,
As guided by Your hand above.
May I not judge, but seek to care,
In every burden they must bear.
With kindness, may I heal the strain,
And bring us close in joy and pain.
Thank You, Lord, for love that binds,
For softening hearts and opening minds.
With faith in You, our love will grow,
In compassion true, we'll always know.

Prayer for Forgiving and Moving Forward

Lord, teach me how to truly forgive,
To let go of pain and let love live.
Help me release each grudge I bear,
And walk in love, with greater care.
Though hurt remains and wounds are deep,
In Your peace, my heart I keep.
Grant me grace to move ahead,
In pathways bright, where love is led.
Forgive us both for wrongs we've done,
And let our hearts be joined as one.
With every step, may peace prevail,
In love renewed, we shall not fail.
Thank You, Lord, for love that heals,
For mending hearts and lifting seals.
With faith in You, I'm free to start,
In joy restored and open heart.

Prayer for Healing Marital Strain

Father, our marriage needs Your grace,
Help us find a peaceful place.
In vows we took, let love renew,
And guide us in what's just and true.
In misunderstandings, let us see,
How Your love can set us free.
Give us patience, help us care,
And lead us to a love that's rare.
Let forgiveness be our guide,
And remove the walls we've built inside.
Strengthen us, as one we stand,
Held together by Your hand.
Thank You, Lord, for love so pure,
For helping our bond to endure.
With faith in You, we're strong again,
In unity, our love sustains.

Prayer for Healing a Parent-Child Relationship

God, our bond feels worn and strained,
From words and actions unrestrained.
Heal the hurt and guide our way,
So love between us will not sway.
Help me see them through Your eyes,
And let compassion fill our ties.
In every word, let patience grow,
So understanding we may know.
Teach me grace and kindness, too,
To let Your love come shining through.
In every moment, let us heal,
With love restored and truth revealed.
Thank You, Lord, for family dear,
For helping us draw closer here.
With faith, we'll build a bond anew,
In love that's deep and ever true.

Prayer for Reconnecting with Loved Ones

Lord, help us find our way again,
To heal the past and make amends.
Where distance grew, let love restore,
And open hearts as never before.
Grant us strength to reach across,
To find what's lost and heal the loss.
Let understanding pave the way,
And guide us back in love today.
With every step, let pride release,
And in its place, bring perfect peace.
Renew our love, refresh our ties,
And let all bitterness subside.
Thank You, Lord, for love so kind,
For bringing healing to heart and mind.
With faith in You, our bond will grow,
In love and grace, together we'll know.

Prayer for Light in Dark Times

Lord, my days feel shrouded in grey,
A darkness that won't go away.
In moments heavy, still and cold,
Hold my heart, let hope unfold.
Shine Your light into my night,
And fill me with Your warming light.
Renew my spirit, lift my soul,
Make every broken part feel whole.
In Your love, may courage grow,
To walk through shadows I don't know.
Thank You, Lord, for love so deep,
In Your peace, my soul will keep.
With hope in You, I rise again,
My faithful God, my closest friend.

Prayer for Strength to Endure

Father, when despair feels near,
Help me find the strength to persevere.
In heavy moments, weary and low,
May Your peace within me grow.
Lift my heart from depths unseen,
Where fear and sadness have been.
Guide me through each passing day,
To find the hope along the way.
Thank You, Lord, for strength so true,
For walking with me, helping me through.
With faith in You, my spirit will mend,
In You, my darkest days shall end.

Prayer for Renewed Purpose

Lord, I feel so lost inside,
Seeking meaning, nowhere to hide.
Help me see beyond this pain,
And find a purpose once again.
In Your love, let courage rise,
Help me see life with new eyes.
Renew my heart, restore my sight,
To walk with hope through every night.
Thank You, God, for guiding me,
For showing purpose yet to be.
With faith in You, I'll rise anew,
In purpose found, my heart is true.

Prayer for Peace Within

God of peace, my heart feels torn,
In sadness, I am weak and worn.
Fill my soul with quiet grace,
And let Your calm take fear's place.
When worries cloud and doubts arise,
Show me hope with clear skies.
Help me find a steady peace,
That all my inner storms may cease.
Thank You, Lord, for peace You give,
For helping me find strength to live.
With faith in You, I stand secure,
And in Your love, my soul is sure.

Prayer for Finding Joy Again

Lord, the joy I knew has faded,
My heart feels lost, dark and jaded.
Restore the laughter once I knew,
And help me find a path to You.
Breathe Your joy into my soul,
Make every broken part feel whole.
With each new day, may joy arise,
And lift my gaze to hopeful skies.
Thank You, Lord, for joy so pure,
For love that helps my heart endure.
With faith in You, I will embrace,
A life of joy, a life of grace.

Prayer for Hope Amidst Despair

Lord, in despair, my heart does cry,
A heavy weight I cannot deny.
But in You, I find a way,
To carry on through each new day.
Help me see beyond the pain,
To find the hope that will sustain.
With each step, renew my will,
And let Your peace my soul fulfil.
Thank You, God, for hope You bring,
For lifting me on broken wings.
With faith, I'll walk through shadowed days,
Until I'm met with brighter rays.

Prayer for Courage to Face Each Day

Father, when courage fades away,
Give me strength to face each day.
Help me rise despite the fears,
And brush away these silent tears.
In every hour, be my guide,
With hope and faith by my side.
Grant me strength to hold my ground,
In love and peace so freely found.
Thank You, Lord, for strength anew,
For helping me to make it through.
With trust in You, I find my way,
To face each new and brighter day.

Prayer for Healing from Sadness

God, this sadness weighs so deep,
My spirit low, I long for peace.
In every tear that falls unseen,
Heal the sorrow in between.
Lift me up with gentle care,
And take this sadness I bear.
Let hope's soft whispers fill my soul,
And make my broken spirit whole.
Thank You, Lord, for love that heals,
For peace and strength that sorrow seals.
With faith in You, I will arise,
And find my light beyond the skies.

Prayer for Resilience and Hope

Lord, help me find resilience here,
When hope feels distant, dark, unclear.
Strengthen me to stand once more,
To open wide a brighter door.
In every trial, may I grow,
With courage deep, so I may know.
Fill me with Your steady light,
To guide me through the longest night.
Thank You, God, for hope within,
For lifting me, my closest kin.
With faith in You, I rise again,
To face the day with love, amen.

Prayer for Finding Peace of Mind

Father, calm my troubled mind,
Help me leave the past behind.
In every thought, let peace reside,
And hold me close, here by Your side.
May I release the fears that bind,
And let Your love renew my mind.
Where shadows linger, may I see,
The light of hope You give to me.
Thank You, Lord, for peace so dear,
For quiet strength to face my fear.
With faith in You, I walk secure,
In peace and joy, my heart is pure.

Prayer for Daily Strength in Weakness

Lord, my strength is frail and worn,
In this body, weary and torn.
Each day brings battles, trials anew,
I place my trust completely in You.
Grant me patience, help me bear,
The constant pain, the endless care.
Fill me with courage, day by day,
To find Your light along the way.
Hold my heart in moments tough,
When life and strength don't feel enough.
With You beside me, I'll stand tall,
For in Your love, I'll never fall.
Thank You, Lord, for strength to cope,
For every breath, for every hope.
With faith, I walk each weary mile,
In You, my heart can rest awhile.

Prayer for Peace in Painful Days

Father, in this chronic pain,
I seek Your peace to break the strain.
When days feel endless, hope seems far,
Be my light, my guiding star.
Help me breathe through every ache,
To find the strength that will not break.
In every moment, remind me true,
That I am safe, held close by You.
Give me patience to endure,
And faith that stands, steady and pure.
In every shadow, let me see,
Your love surrounding, holding me.
Thank You, Lord, for strength each day,
For guiding me along the way.
With faith in You, I'll face each fight,
In endless love, my soul's delight.

Prayer for Hope Through Long Suffering

Lord, this journey feels so long,
The days are hard, the nights feel wrong.
In my suffering, grant me peace,
And let Your presence never cease.
Fill my heart with hopeful light,
Guide me through each painful night.
Though illness lingers, I hold on,
To the promise of Your dawn.
Help me find joy within the strain,
And peace amid the constant pain.
With You, my courage is restored,
In every trial, my strength assured.
Thank You, Lord, for love so vast,
For peace that helps my spirit last.
With faith, I rise above the fray,
In Your care, my fears allay.

Prayer for Resilience in the Journey

God, each step feels hard to take,
With strength so frail, with body weak.
Grant me resilience to face this path,
And comfort me through pain and wrath.
May every breath renew my soul,
And make each broken part feel whole.
In moments where I feel undone,
Remind me, Lord, that You've already won.
Help me hold on through the strain,
To find Your peace within my pain.
In You, my strength will never fail,
Through every storm, through every gale.
Thank You, Lord, for staying near,
For lifting burdens, calming fear.
With faith in You, I'll face each test,
In Your embrace, I find my rest.

Prayer for Endurance in Hardship

Lord, my days are long and trying,
In moments weak, I feel like crying.
Grant me endurance to stand firm,
And in Your love, help me learn.
To face each day with strength anew,
To know my hope is found in You.
Let each trial build me strong,
Through every ache, to carry on.
Guide me with patience, calm my mind,
And let Your peace be what I find.
For in my weakness, You are near,
And in Your love, I feel no fear.
Thank You, God, for strength to last,
For helping me to hold steadfast.
With faith in You, my spirit's high,
And in Your grace, I will not die.

Prayer for Grace to Accept My Struggles

Father, I struggle with this load,
A constant, wearying, heavy road.
Help me find grace to accept my way,
And strength to live through each new day.
Though illness claims much of me,
In You, my heart can still be free.
Grant me patience, steady and calm,
And fill my soul with healing balm.
Teach me to rest in all I lack,
For in Your love, there's no turning back.
With every breath, renew my soul,
And make this broken spirit whole.
Thank You, Lord, for grace so deep,
For every promise You keep.
With faith, I rise to face each hour,
Held and healed by Your mighty power.

Prayer for Strength to Trust in God's Plan

God, this illness wears me down,
In weakness, I feel like I might drown.
But in Your plan, I'll trust and stand,
Knowing You hold me in Your hand.
Help me lean on Your design,
And know my life is truly Thine.
Though I may not see the way,
Your guidance is my hope today.
With faith that You know what's best,
I lay my weary soul to rest.
Let every moment bring me peace,
As I trust in Your sweet release.
Thank You, Lord, for guiding me,
Through every storm, through every sea.
With faith in You, my soul is bright,
In Your love, I find my light.

Prayer for Comfort in Long Nights

Father, the nights feel cold and long,
Where is my strength? Where is my song?
In every silent, weary hour,
I seek the comfort of Your power.
Help me feel Your warmth so near,
To drive away each aching fear.
Fill my heart with peace and rest,
As I lean upon Your chest.
Through endless nights and darkened skies,
Be the love that never dies.
With every tear, draw close to me,
In Your embrace, I'm truly free.
Thank You, Lord, for nights You soothe,
For bringing calm, for peace renewed.
With faith, I'll rise, no longer weak,
In You, my rest is what I seek.

Prayer for Finding Joy Amidst Pain

God, help me see beyond the pain,
To find the joy that will remain.
In every struggle, help me see,
The blessings that You give to me.
Though pain is constant, let me find,
The joy that's lasting, pure, and kind.
With every smile, let strength renew,
And let my spirit rest in You.
Help me laugh and live each day,
With faith and love that won't decay.
In every sorrow, teach me peace,
And let my joy and strength increase.
Thank You, Lord, for joy so sweet,
For helping me stand on steady feet.
With faith in You, my spirit soars,
And joy is mine forevermore.

Prayer for Finding Peace in Illness

Lord, this illness brings much pain,
With fears I cannot quite contain.
Help me find Your peace, so near,
And calm each worry, calm each fear.
In every struggle, help me see,
Your gentle hand, guiding me.
Let peace be found in every breath,
As I trust Your love beyond all death.
Teach me to rest in what You give,
And find true peace, that I may live.
Though health may falter, You remain,
My constant peace, my strength in pain.
Thank You, Lord, for peace so sure,
For grace that helps me to endure.
With faith in You, my heart will rest,
In Your peace, I am truly blessed.

Prayer for Letting Go of Guilt

Lord, the guilt I carry is deep,
A burden heavy, hard to keep.
Help me release this weight I bear,
And find forgiveness through Your care.
Teach me grace to see anew,
That Your mercy, Lord, is true.
In Your love, may I let go,
Of past regrets and wounds I know.
Heal my heart, renew my soul,
Make every broken part feel whole.
Teach me to love myself again,
With peace restored and free from sin.
Thank You, Lord, for grace so wide,
For holding me close, right by my side.
In Your love, I'm free at last,
My guilt and shame are in the past.

Prayer for Embracing Self-Compassion

Father, help me see with love,
The grace You offer from above.
Teach me compassion for my heart,
To love each imperfect part.
May I release each harsh regret,
And learn to live without a threat.
In every moment, let me find,
A love that's patient, pure, and kind.
Guide me to forgive my flaws,
And find in me a holy cause.
In Your love, I see my worth,
As a child of light, reborn on earth.
Thank You, Lord, for love so true,
For teaching me to love me too.
With faith in You, I'm whole again,
In self-compassion, free from pain.

Prayer for Accepting God's Forgiveness

Lord, I seek forgiveness now,
To release the guilt I can't allow.
Help me trust Your mercy deep,
And find in You my soul's true peace.
Though I am flawed, You love me still,
In every way, by Your will.
May I accept the grace You give,
And find the freedom so to live.
Teach me to trust Your holy love,
Forgiveness sent from up above.
In Your light, I find my way,
Released from shame, to face the day.
Thank You, God, for mercy wide,
For love that never runs or hides.
In Your forgiveness, I am free,
To love myself as You love me.

Prayer for Release from Self-Judgment

Father, my heart is hard and cold,
In self-judgment, I am sold.
Help me find a gentler place,
To live my life within Your grace.
Teach me to release each thought,
That traps me in what I am not.
In Your love, I see what's true,
That I am cherished, loved by You.
Help me see with kinder eyes,
Beyond my faults, beyond disguise.
May self-forgiveness fill my heart,
In Your peace, I find my part.
Thank You, Lord, for love so kind,
For freeing me from chains that bind.
With faith in You, I live again,
Released from judgment, freed from pain.

Prayer for Healing from Regret

God, regret weighs on my mind,
Memories painful, unrefined.
Help me let go, to find release,
And guide my soul to perfect peace.
In Your love, I lay them down,
Each regret and shameful frown.
Help me see that I am more,
A spirit loved, forever pure.
Teach me grace to let it be,
And find in You serenity.
May each memory fade away,
As peace and love within me stay.
Thank You, Lord, for love so strong,
For healing me where I've done wrong.
With faith in You, I let go now,
And in Your peace, I humbly bow.

Prayer for Forgiving My Mistakes

Lord, my mistakes haunt my soul,
Making me feel less than whole.
Help me forgive the things I've done,
And see I'm loved, Your chosen one.
Teach me grace to love anew,
And see my worth as You do too.
With each mistake, let wisdom grow,
And guide my steps in ways to show.
In Your love, I am redeemed,
Worthy of the dreams I dreamed.
Grant me peace to live unbound,
In self-forgiveness, freedom found.
Thank You, Lord, for love so pure,
For helping me my soul secure.
With faith in You, I'm free to live,
In grace and peace, I can forgive.

Prayer for Embracing My True Worth

Father, help me see my worth,
As a child of light here on earth.
Guide me past the lies I hear,
That fill my heart with shame and fear.
In Your love, I am complete,
With every flaw, I am unique.
Help me accept the love You give,
To embrace myself, to truly live.
Let self-forgiveness fill my soul,
And make each broken part feel whole.
In Your light, I stand secure,
With faith and love forever sure.
Thank You, Lord, for love so true,
For helping me see myself anew.
With faith in You, I find my place,
In self-acceptance, pure in grace.

Prayer for Releasing Shame and Embracing Grace

Lord, shame has bound me long and tight,
Blocking peace, obscuring light.
Help me see with softened eyes,
The grace You give, so vast, so wise.
May I release the shame I bear,
And live my life in holy care.
In Your love, I'll find my peace,
And let my burdens gently cease.
Teach me how to truly see,
The grace You pour so lovingly.
Let self-forgiveness take its place,
And fill my heart with healing grace.
Thank You, Lord, for freeing me,
For lifting shame, for helping me see.
With faith in You, my spirit's bright,
In Your love, I find my light.

Prayer for Healing the Heart's Wounds

Father, my heart carries wounds so deep,
Moments I cannot seem to keep.
Heal each scar, mend each pain,
And let self-love within me reign.
Help me forgive the parts I hide,
And see myself through loving eyes.
In Your peace, let healing flow,
So in Your grace, I'll truly know.
May I love myself anew,
As Your love makes all things true.
Teach me, Lord, to stand in peace,
And find in You my sweet release.
Thank You, God, for love so near,
For quieting every shameful fear.
With faith in You, my heart is whole,
Forgiven and free in heart and soul.

Prayer for Peace Within Myself

Lord, I long for peace inside,
To let go of all I've tried to hide.
Teach me to forgive my soul,
And trust in You to make me whole.
In every fault, let mercy reign,
To ease my heart of guilt and pain.
May I live with peace so true,
Held in love that comes from You.
In Your grace, I find my way,
To love myself more each day.
Let self-forgiveness be my light,
And guide me through each silent night.
Thank You, Lord, for peace so deep,
For helping me my soul to keep.
With faith in You, my heart will mend,
And find in peace a lifelong friend.

Prayer for Wisdom in Times of Uncertainty

Lord, I stand at a crossroads today,
Unsure of the steps along my way.
Grant me wisdom, pure and true,
To see the path I should pursue.
Open my heart to trust in You,
When decisions are hard and answers few.
Let Your guidance light my way,
And lead me safely, day by day.
In times of doubt, let faith arise,
To see my future through Your eyes.
Help me listen, help me hear,
Your gentle voice so calm and clear.
Thank You, Lord, for wisdom's gift,
For steady hands when choices shift.
With faith in You, I'll find my way,
In trust and peace, I'll walk each day.

Prayer for Clarity in Confusion

Father, my mind is clouded and weak,
With questions and doubts, I struggle to seek.
Clear the fog that blurs my sight,
And guide me, Lord, with holy light.
Teach me patience to wait for You,
To know what's right, to see what's true.
Let clarity in my spirit reign,
And help me choose without disdain.
May my heart be open wide,
To trust in You, my constant guide.
Give me peace in every choice,
And help me hear Your guiding voice.
Thank You, Lord, for light anew,
For showing me what's good and true.
With faith in You, I'll make my choice,
In quiet trust, I hear Your voice.

Prayer for Guidance in Uncharted Paths

Lord, the road ahead feels strange,
Full of choices, new and strange.
Guide me through each unknown part,
With courage and a willing heart.
In every decision, big or small,
Help me trust that You know all.
Though I may not see the end,
Your wisdom guides me, friend to friend.
Grant me strength to walk with grace,
To trust in every step I face.
With You, I know I will not stray,
For You are with me, come what may.
Thank You, Lord, for every guide,
For leading me, close by my side.
With faith in You, I'm safe and sound,
In Your love, my path is found.

Prayer for Courage to Choose

Father, decisions weigh me down,
Leaving my heart to fret and frown.
Grant me courage to make a stand,
With strength that comes from Your hand.
Help me trust in what is right,
To walk with faith, to find Your light.
In every choice, may I find peace,
And let my anxious worries cease.
Though fear may come, let courage stay,
As I trust in You each day.
Guide my thoughts and steady my soul,
And help me reach my highest goal.
Thank You, Lord, for courage deep,
For helping me my peace to keep.
With faith in You, I choose my way,
In Your strength, I'll face each day.

Prayer for Trust in God's Direction

Lord, I don't know what lies ahead,
With paths uncertain, filled with dread.
Help me trust in what You plan,
And place my future in Your hand.
Teach me to walk with open heart,
And know that You will do Your part.
Though unknown roads may feel unsure,
In You, my path is safe and pure.
Let faith arise, dispel my fear,
For in Your love, I know You're near.
Guide me, Lord, in all I do,
And help me trust my steps to You.
Thank You, Lord, for wisdom's light,
For guiding me through darkest night.
With faith, I'll walk, my trust in Thee,
In Your love, I am free.

Prayer for Discernment and Insight

Father, I seek discernment true,
To see each choice with eyes from You.
Help me find the path You've laid,
With clarity that does not fade.
In each decision, help me see,
The path of peace, the way to be.
Let insight guide my every thought,
In every choice that must be sought.
Teach me patience, keep me still,
To know and follow Your holy will.
With every choice, may I be wise,
In trust that never compromises.
Thank You, Lord, for insight pure,
For helping me my steps secure.
With faith in You, my path is clear,
In peace and strength, I have no fear.

Prayer for Patience in Decision-Making

Lord, I need patience to decide,
To wait and not be swept aside.
Help me pause and seek Your voice,
In every hard and pressing choice.
Teach me wisdom to delay,
And let Your peace show me the way.
In moments rushed, keep me still,
And let me know Your gentle will.
Guide my heart to wait in peace,
Until the answers You release.
In every choice, help me find grace,
And trust Your timing, steady pace.
Thank You, Lord, for patience true,
For leading me as I wait on You.
With faith, I'll stand, calm and strong,
In Your love, where I belong.

Prayer for Clear Vision and Purpose

Father, I seek a vision bright,
To see each step with guided light.
Help me find my purpose clear,
And follow paths that bring me near.
In every choice, reveal the way,
That leads to peace and joy each day.
With Your vision, let me see,
The path You've set ahead for me.
Give me wisdom, calm, and grace,
To walk each step at my own pace.
In Your love, I place my trust,
And follow where Your Spirit must.
Thank You, Lord, for vision pure,
For helping me to stand secure.
With faith in You, I find my call,
In Your purpose, I am whole.

Prayer for Guidance Through Doubt

Lord, doubt surrounds me, clouds my mind,
In every thought, no peace I find.
Help me see beyond my fear,
And know that You are ever near.
Grant me faith when doubt is strong,
To choose what's right, to know what's wrong.
In every step, let wisdom reign,
And help me walk in love again.
Guide me through uncertain times,
With peace that knows no bounds or lines.
Teach me trust in Your embrace,
To walk with calm, with steady pace.
Thank You, Lord, for peace in doubt,
For leading me when I'm without.
With faith in You, my fears will cease,
In You, I find my lasting peace.

Prayer for Faith in God's Plan

Father, Your plans are great and sure,
In them, my future is secure.
Help me trust in what You see,
And know You hold the best for me.
Though choices come and doubts appear,
Guide my heart and calm my fear.
Help me walk with steady faith,
To trust Your goodness, know Your grace.
With every choice, help me be wise,
To follow where Your wisdom lies.
In Your love, I place my hope,
For in Your arms, I am not alone.
Thank You, Lord, for plans so true,
For guiding me in all I do.
With faith in You, my future's bright,
In Your love, I walk in light.

Prayer for Peace in the Midst of Grief

Lord, my heart is heavy with pain,
From loss so deep, it feels like rain.
In this sorrow, be my peace,
And let my restless heart find release.
Hold me close in this time of tears,
Guide me through my deepest fears.
Bring comfort to my wounded soul,
And make my broken spirit whole.
Help me honour memories dear,
And feel Your presence ever near.
Though grief may stay, let peace arise,
And lift my gaze toward hopeful skies.
Thank You, Lord, for love's embrace,
For holding me in this quiet place.
With faith in You, I'll find my way,
Through every tear, each darkened day.

Prayer for Strength to Face Each Day

Father, each day feels hard to bear,
Without the loved one who's no longer there.
Grant me strength to face each dawn,
To carry on though they are gone.
Help me find the courage strong,
To honour them, to carry on.
In Your love, let strength abide,
And help me hold to hope inside.
Though I grieve, let me not fall,
For in Your grace, I stand tall.
With every breath, let healing start,
And mend the pieces of my heart.
Thank You, Lord, for strength anew,
For guiding me as I trust in You.
With faith, I'll rise and walk once more,
In love and peace, forevermore.

Prayer for Comfort in Times of Sorrow

Lord, sorrow fills my heart with ache,
In waves of grief, I feel it break.
Come near and hold my trembling hand,
And guide me to a peaceful land.
In Your love, I seek release,
To find some comfort, gentle peace.
Let every tear I shed be seen,
And heal the wounds that lie between.
Help me cherish memories sweet,
To find in love a soft retreat.
Though loss may linger, love remains,
A soothing balm for all my pains.
Thank You, Lord, for comfort's light,
For holding me through every night.
With faith in You, I find my way,
And lean on You, come what may.

Prayer for Restoring Joy After Loss

Father, my joy feels far away,
Lost in the shadows of yesterday.
Renew my heart, bring joy anew,
And guide me closer, Lord, to You.
Though I mourn, let laughter bloom,
To light the darkness of this gloom.
Teach me to find moments bright,
To live in love, to walk in light.
With every memory cherished near,
Help me feel Your presence here.
In loss and love, let joy survive,
To remind me that I am alive.
Thank You, Lord, for joy restored,
For lifting sorrow, for being my Lord.
With faith in You, I'll live and see,
That love is here eternally.

Prayer for Healing in the Wake of Loss

Lord, my heart is bruised and sore,
From loss that shakes me to the core.
In Your peace, let healing flow,
And comfort me as grief I know.
Teach me patience as I heal,
And in Your love, my soul reveal.
Through every tear and whispered prayer,
Help me know that You are there.
Guide me through the pain I feel,
To find a hope that's strong and real.
Though grief may stay, let love increase,
And bring my heart to perfect peace.
Thank You, Lord, for healing's grace,
For holding me in this quiet space.
With faith in You, my soul is free,
In love and hope, eternally.

Prayer for Remembering with Love

Father, memories flood my mind,
Of days with love and joy entwined.
Help me honour those I miss,
And cherish them with every kiss.
Teach me how to hold them near,
In ways that bring me peace, not fear.
Let love remain, a bridge so true,
Between my heart and those with You.
Guide me in my grief's embrace,
To find a calm, a sacred place.
For though they're gone, their love remains,
To comfort me through all my pains.
Thank You, Lord, for memories sweet,
For keeping loved ones close, complete.
With faith, I know they're not far,
In Your love, they're where You are.

Prayer for Finding Hope in Loss

Lord, in loss, my hope feels small,
A distant light, a faint recall.
Bring me closer, help me see,
That hope still lives inside of me.
In every tear and painful thought,
Remind me, Lord, I am not forgot.
Help me trust in what will be,
To find my peace and strength in Thee.
Though grief may linger in my soul,
Let hope renew and make me whole.
Guide me with Your loving hand,
To trust in things I may not understand.
Thank You, Lord, for hope anew,
For guiding me as I lean on You.
With faith, I walk with love to see,
That hope and joy are meant for me.

Prayer for Peaceful Remembrance

Father, bring me peace today,
As I remember in this quiet way.
Help me honour memories dear,
With love and comfort, ever near.
Let not sorrow cloud my view,
But bring me joy in memories true.
Teach me to cherish every part,
Of those who linger in my heart.
Guide me gently, show me peace,
As grief within begins to cease.
In Your love, let memories grow,
And help me find the strength to go.
Thank You, Lord, for love's pure grace,
For holding me in this sacred space.
With faith, I walk this path of light,
With loved ones near, though out of sight.

Prayer for Healing the Heart's Ache

Lord, my heart aches with love's loss,
A heavy burden, a weighty cross.
Hold me close in sorrow's night,
And fill my soul with healing light.
In moments where I feel undone,
Remind me, Lord, that love lives on.
Guide my heart to find release,
And bring my spirit gentle peace.
Though grief may stay, let love endure,
In memories sweet, in feelings pure.
With every breath, let healing flow,
To mend the wounds that sorrow sows.
Thank You, Lord, for healing's hand,
For helping me to understand.
With faith, I'll find my way again,
In love's sweet light, I'll find my friend.

Prayer for Strength in the Journey of Grief

Father, this grief feels hard and long,
A journey where I must be strong.
Grant me strength to carry through,
To hold to love and rest in You.
Help me find the path ahead,
To honour those who've gone instead.
In every memory, let peace grow,
And teach me all I need to know.
Guide me through the pain I bear,
With comfort found in holy prayer.
Though loss may linger, love is here,
To light my way and calm my fear.
Thank You, Lord, for strength You give,
For helping me to truly live.
With faith, I walk this road so deep,
In peace and love, my soul will keep.

Prayer for Rediscovering Joy

Lord, my heart feels empty, cold,
My joy seems lost, my spirit old.
Awaken within me a spark so bright,
To fill my soul with renewed delight.
Help me find joy in simple things,
In morning light and birds that sing.
Show me wonder in each day,
And guide my steps along the way.
Let laughter bloom, let hope arise,
As I see life through joyful eyes.
With every moment, let me see,
Your grace and beauty surrounding me.
Thank You, Lord, for joy restored,
For filling my life with sweet reward.
With faith in You, my spirit sings,
And joy within my heart takes wing.

Prayer for Purpose in Uncertain Times

Father, my path feels blurred and grey,
I long for purpose to light my way.
Reveal the steps that I should take,
And guide me, Lord, for my soul's sake.
In each new day, let vision grow,
To see the plans You've yet to show.
Grant me courage to believe,
That purpose waits, if I'll receive.
Help me trust Your perfect will,
To walk with faith, to wait and still.
In every task, let joy abide,
With purpose found, my steadfast guide.
Thank You, Lord, for purpose true,
For dreams revived and strength anew.
With faith in You, I find my place,
In joy and purpose, through Your grace.

Prayer for Renewed Enthusiasm for Life

Lord, I need a spark inside,
A passion I no longer hide.
Fill me with zeal, with life anew,
To live with joy, to honour You.
Help me find delight again,
In things I love, in family, friends.
Restore my will, my energy,
To live my life abundantly.
Grant me strength to chase my dreams,
To know that life is more than it seems.
With every breath, let purpose grow,
And fill my heart with love's warm glow.
Thank You, Lord, for dreams that rise,
For filling me with new supplies.
With faith in You, my joy is clear,
In purpose found, You're always near.

Prayer for Discovering New Dreams

Father, I feel lost inside,
With dreams long gone, with hopes denied.
Give me courage to dream once more,
To open wide life's hidden door.
Show me new paths I can take,
And guide me in decisions I make.
Let each step reveal a way,
To bring me joy in work and play.
Help me find my passion true,
In everything I'm called to do.
With each new goal, let purpose shine,
As I follow Your design.
Thank You, Lord, for dreams anew,
For helping me see life's view.
With faith, I step into my call,
With purpose clear, I give my all.

Prayer for Joy in Small Moments

Lord, help me see with eyes so bright,
The joy in every day and night.
Teach me to love the little things,
And find delight in life's small wings.
In each laugh and tender smile,
Let joy abound, if just a while.
In simple tasks and quiet days,
Help me see Your loving ways.
Let my heart be light and free,
To find joy abundantly.
Fill my soul with peace and cheer,
And help me know that You are near.
Thank You, Lord, for joy so small,
That lifts my heart and breaks my fall.
With faith in You, I'll always see,
The joy that's here surrounding me.

Prayer for Purpose Beyond Myself

Father, show me ways to serve,
To give my all with steady nerve.
Help me see beyond my need,
To help a world that's hard to feed.
Let purpose fill me through and through,
In everything I say and do.
Teach me love, let kindness flow,
And help me bring joy where I go.
In every action, let me find,
A purpose pure and love so kind.
With each step, let my life show,
A heart that's blessed, a soul aglow.
Thank You, Lord, for purpose clear,
For showing me why I'm here.
With faith in You, my soul's alive,
In purpose strong, I truly thrive.

Prayer for New Energy and Zeal

Lord, my strength feels weak and worn,
Help me rise, each day reborn.
Grant me energy, vibrant and true,
To live with passion, close to You.
In every task, give strength to try,
With zeal renewed, to reach and fly.
In every day, let purpose grow,
And fill my heart with love's warm glow.
Give me courage to pursue,
The goals and dreams I hold from You.
With every step, may I proclaim,
The joy of living in Your name.
Thank You, Lord, for strength and cheer,
For showing me my purpose clear.
With faith in You, my life is bright,
In joy and purpose, love's pure light.

Prayer for Joy to Overcome Doubt

Father, doubt has clouded me,
Making joy so hard to see.
Help me trust in what's to come,
To know my life's not yet done.
Guide me through uncertain days,
And show me light in quiet ways.
Let joy return with every breath,
And lead me through the fears of death.
Teach me to laugh, to hope, to dream,
To know my life is more than it seems.
With purpose found, let joy reside,
And be my light, my faithful guide.
Thank You, Lord, for joy that's clear,
For lifting doubt, for drawing near.
With faith in You, I'm born anew,
In joy and hope, forever true.

Prayer for Purpose in the Present Moment

Lord, I seek a purpose here,
In every hour, in each year.
Help me find what's meant for me,
In every task and moment free.
Teach me joy in what I do,
In tasks that seem both old and new.
Let each moment show me why,
I'm here on earth, beneath the sky.
Help me see that life's not small,
But filled with purpose, filled with call.
In each breath, let meaning rise,
As I live my life with open eyes.
Thank You, Lord, for purpose near,
For helping me see life so clear.
With faith in You, I find my call,
In every moment, big and small.

Prayer for Finding Joy in Serving Others

Father, help me live to give,
To bring joy to others while I live.
Let my purpose be to serve,
With kindness bold, with steady nerve.
In every act, may joy increase,
To spread Your love, to bring them peace.
Let purpose drive me every day,
In each small task, along the way.
Help me find the joy in giving,
To make my life one worth living.
With love that grows in work and play,
Let service guide me every day.
Thank You, Lord, for joy that's found,
In serving all the world around.
With faith in You, I walk secure,
In purpose true and love so pure.

Disclaimer

The prayers and reflections in this book, Prayers for Healing, are intended to provide spiritual support, comfort, and inspiration. They are not a substitute for professional medical, psychological, or therapeutic care. If you or someone you know is experiencing a health crisis, chronic illness, mental health challenge, or any other medical or psychological concern, please seek guidance from a qualified healthcare provider or mental health professional.

While these prayers are crafted to encourage hope and healing, they are designed to complement—not replace—any professional treatment, counselling, or medical advice you may require. Each individual's healing journey is unique, and the path to wellness often involves a blend of faith, self-care, and professional support.

The author and publisher of this book do not assume responsibility for any personal outcomes or decisions made based on the content provided herein. May these prayers offer peace, comfort, and strength, enhancing your journey alongside the care and support you receive.

Milton Keynes UK
Ingram Content Group UK Ltd.
UKHW030853151124
451262UK00001B/188